Muriel Stanek

I SPEAK ENGLISH
FOR MY MOM

Illustrations by Judith Friedman

Albert Whitman & Company • Morton Grove, Illinois

Text © 1989 by Muriel Stanek.
Illustrations © 1989 by Judith Friedman.
Published in 1989 by Albert Whitman & Company,
    6340 Oakton Street, Morton Grove, Illinois 60053.
Published simultaneously in Canada by
    Fitzhenry & Whiteside, Markham, Ontario.
Printed in the United States of America.
20 19 18 17 16 15 14 13 12

Library of Congress Cataloging-in-Publication Data

Stanek, Muriel.
    I speak English for my mom / Muriel Stanek;
Illustrated by Judith Friedman.

p. cm.
    Summary: Lupe, a young Mexican American, must
translate for her mother, who speaks only Spanish,
until Mrs. Gomez decides to learn English in order to
get a better job.
    ISBN 0-8075-3659-8 (lib.bdg.)
[1. Mexican Americans—Fiction. 2. Mothers and
daughters—Fiction.] I. Friedman, Judith, 1945-
ill. II. Title.
PZ7.S78637Ias 1989   88-20546
[FIC]—dc19
                                                         CIP
                                                         AC

For Natalie. M.S.
Muchas gracias, Patricia, Sonia, y Artemio. J.F.

When I was small, Mom helped me do everything. Now that I'm older, I have to help my mom because I can speak English, and she can't.

At school I use English all the time.
At home Mom and I speak Spanish together.
And outside our home, I speak for her.

If a stranger says something to Mom in English,
she quickly asks, "*¿Qué dijo?*"
which means "What did he say?"
I tell her in Spanish
and then answer for her in English.
I feel grown-up.

"What would I do without you, Lupe!" my mother says.
"You are a very good helper."

When Mom takes me to the clinic for my checkup,
the doctor speaks English. I tell Mom what he says.
Once I played a trick on her.
"What did the doctor say?" Mom asked.
"He said I should eat lots of candy and ice cream."
Mom laughed. She knew I was fooling her.

At our school a parent must meet with
the teacher to get the child's report card.
My teacher does not speak Spanish,
so I go to the meeting and tell my mother and
Mrs. Wells what each one is saying.
Mom likes Mrs. Wells because she says I work hard.
"*Muchas gracias*," Mom says to her.
That means, "many thanks."

On the way home, we stop at a Mexican restaurant.
It is my reward for getting a good report card.
Our neighbors the Garcías are there, too.
Carlos and Claudia García are my best friends.
The grown-ups speak Spanish to one another.
The kids and I mix up English and Spanish
while we eat ice cream and tell jokes.

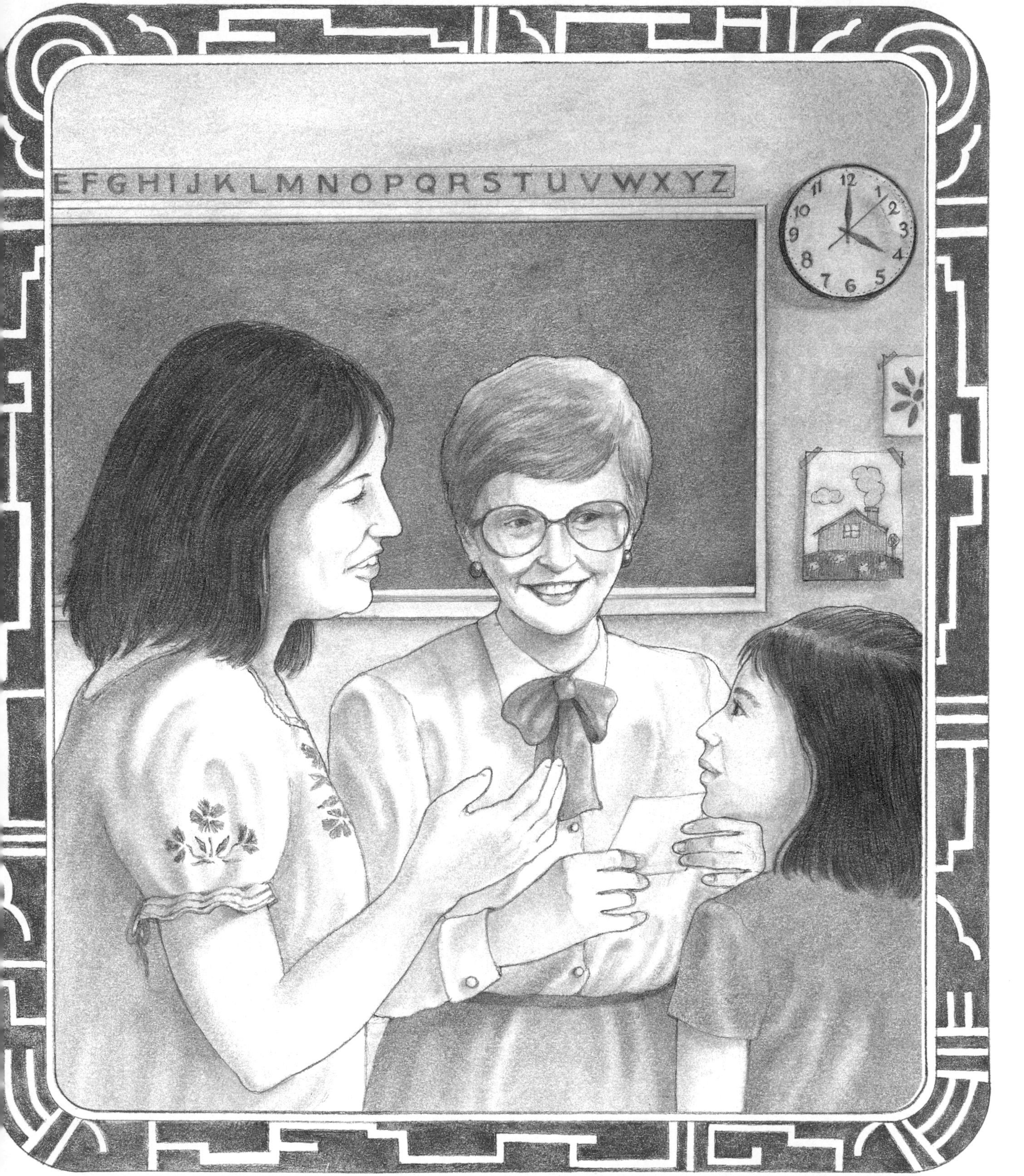
EFGHIJKLMNOPQRSTUVWXYZ

At home we have a telephone.

But we don't use it often because it costs too much.

When the phone rings, I answer it.

If someone is speaking English, I take the message.

I help Mom with the mail, too.

If a letter is written in English,

I read it to her.

Mom reads letters written in Spanish.

Every day my mother goes to work
in a factory in our neighborhood. She sews dresses.
Her boss and all the workers speak Spanish.

On Fridays Mom gets paid, and she cashes her check
at a currency exchange next to the factory.
Everyone there speaks Spanish.
After supper we count the money together and pay the bills.
If any money is left, we save it in a red tin can.

"You should put the money in the bank," I tell Mom.
"No," says Mom, "I'm not ready for that."
I think Mom worries she won't understand what people
at the bank are saying, even if I'm there to help her.

At the supermarket, we pay our electric and gas bills.
I read labels on cans and boxes that don't have pictures,
and then we carry the groceries home.

Mom likes to shop at a little Mexican store on our street.
She doesn't need my help there.
Everybody speaks Spanish,
and the cans and boxes have Spanish labels.

Sometimes I don't want to speak for my mother.
I'd rather be with my friends.
One time I was playing jump rope with Graciela and Julie
when Mom came home early from work
with a terrible toothache.

"You will have to come and speak for me," Mom said.
"I must go to the clinic and see a dentist right away!"
"But I want to play," I told her.
"*¡Necesito que vengas ahora!*" my mother said,
which means, "I need you to come now!"
I wished I didn't have to go with her that day.

Sometimes in the evening, Mom and I just sit and talk.
She likes to tell me how we came from Mexico when I was a baby.
"Your Papa always wanted us to come here," she says,
"but he got very sick. Before he died, he told me,
'Take Lupe to the United States where she can go to college
and get a good job when she grows up.'"

I finish the story for Mom. "And that is why
we must always work hard—so Papa's wish will come true."
Mom smiles because she knows
I have heard this story many times.

On Friday when Mom comes home from work,
she is very worried.
"What's the matter?" I ask.
"Business is not good at our factory," she says.
"Everyone got a cut in pay."

When we count the money that night,
there is just enough to pay the bills.
There's nothing extra for the red can.
"Are we poor?" I ask Mom.
"No," she answers, "but I must find a better job.
Soon you will need a new winter coat and boots."

"You are a good worker," I tell her. "You can get
a better job downtown in a big factory."
"But I need to know English to work downtown,"
Mom says. "Maybe no one will know Spanish in a new place,
and you wouldn't be there to speak for me."

Early Saturday morning we load my wagon with laundry
and go to the laundromat.
On the way we see a long line of people outside the church.
They are waiting to get free food.
"Will we be able to buy food if you lose your job?" I ask.
"Yes," says Mom, "I will always find a way to take care of you."

But I worry what might happen if Mom is out of work.

Inside the laundromat, Mom meets her friend Mrs. Cruz.
They talk about what they will do if the factory closes next year.
Mom looks at the Spanish bulletin board
to see if there are any better jobs in the neighborhood.
There are none.

Then she sees a sign that says free English classes
will be starting next week at the high school.
Mrs. Cruz reads the sign, too.
Mom says they might get better jobs if they learn English.
Mrs. Cruz says she will go to night school if Mom goes with her.
"I will think about it," Mom says.

Late that night, I wake up.
I hear Mom walking back and forth in the kitchen.
"What's the matter?" I call. "Are you sick?"
"No," she says. "I'm worried about night school.
What if I can't fill out the forms? Maybe I can't learn English!"
"Don't worry," I say. "I'll go with you when you
sign up for the class. And you'll learn. You're very smart!"

Mom gives me a hug.
"*Tú eres una niña muy buena,*" she says,
which means "You are a very good girl."
I say, "Papa would be proud of you
because you will make his wish come true."
"Papa would be proud of both of us," she tells me.

Now every Tuesday and Thursday evening,
I stay at Claudia's house while my mother is at school.
Afterward Mom tells me about her English class,
and I help her with her homework.

We are beginning to speak a little English to each other.
I say to Mom, "How do you do? What is your name?"
Mom answers in English,
"I am fine, thank you. My name is Rosa Gómez."
"Where do you live?" I ask.
She says, "I live in Chicago, Illinois."
"Do you have any children?"
"Yes, I have one daughter. Her name is Lupe."
"Very good," I tell her.
"Thank you very much," she says.

Then we go back to speaking Spanish.
"It takes a long time to learn a new language," Mom says.
"But one day you won't have to speak for me anymore."
"I think maybe I will miss it," I tell her.

Mom tucks me into bed.
"*Buenas noches*," I say to her.
"Good night," says Mom.